ISLA OLSEN

Love & Luck

The Adult Coloring Book vol.1

ILLUSTRATED BY ARNILD ALDEPOLLA

Love & Luck

THE ADULT COLORING BOOK VOL. 1

All Artwork by Arnild Aldepolla

Formatting by We Got You Covered Book Design
WWW.WEGOTYOUCOVEREDBOOKDESIGN.COM

FAKE IT 'til You MAKE OUT

"Yup!" I flash her a bright grin. "I'm all for the dick now. I swallow cum and everything—it's delicious."

FAKE IT 'til you
MAKE OUT

"I researched some hashtags on Instagram and those are the type of photos couples post . . ."

FAKE IT 'til you MAKE OUT

His hands on me feel better than I could have possibly imagined, and when he swipes his tongue over the tip it takes every ounce of willpower I possess not to come then and there.

FAKE IT 'til you MAKE OUT

Fuck, he's so sexy; lying out before me like this, his face flushed with the pleasure I'm giving him, his cut cock hard and thick and glistening with precum as it slaps against his abs with each thrust I make. And the noises he's making . . . fuck, I could listen to them all goddamn day.

FAKE IT 'til you MAKE OUT

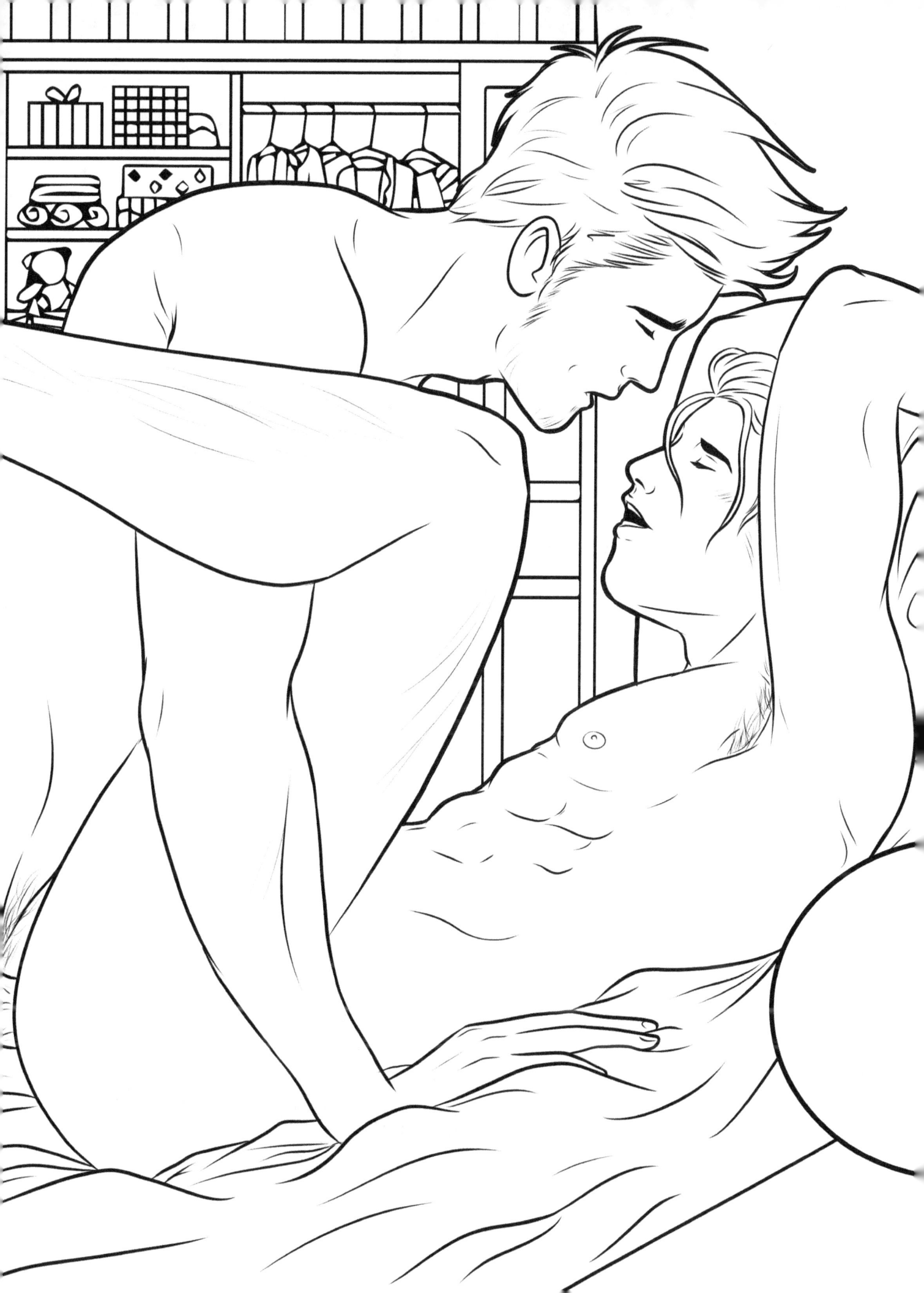

I push in slowly, savoring the sensation of having Declan wrapped around me. When I bottom out, Declan calls, "Fuck me, Heath—don't hold back, baby."

FAKE IT *'til you* **MAKE OUT**

"Okay, maybe when we're telling the story of how we got engaged we could skip the part about my dick being inside you at the time."

Heath offers me a sly smirk. "Or we could show people a picture of it? Then they'll understand why I said yes."

FAKE IT 'til you MAKE OUT

"Okay, so that was a little weird—you *thanked* her?"

"Baby, do you realize if she hadn't posted that thing on Facebook we might not be together right now?"

FAKE IT 'til you MAKE OUT

Any notions I had of this being wrong or inappropriate are pretty quickly forgotten once we start because, yeah, it does feel fucking good. It's just jerking off, sure, but that sexy voice murmuring in my ear and spurring me on while I do it just brings it to a whole new level.

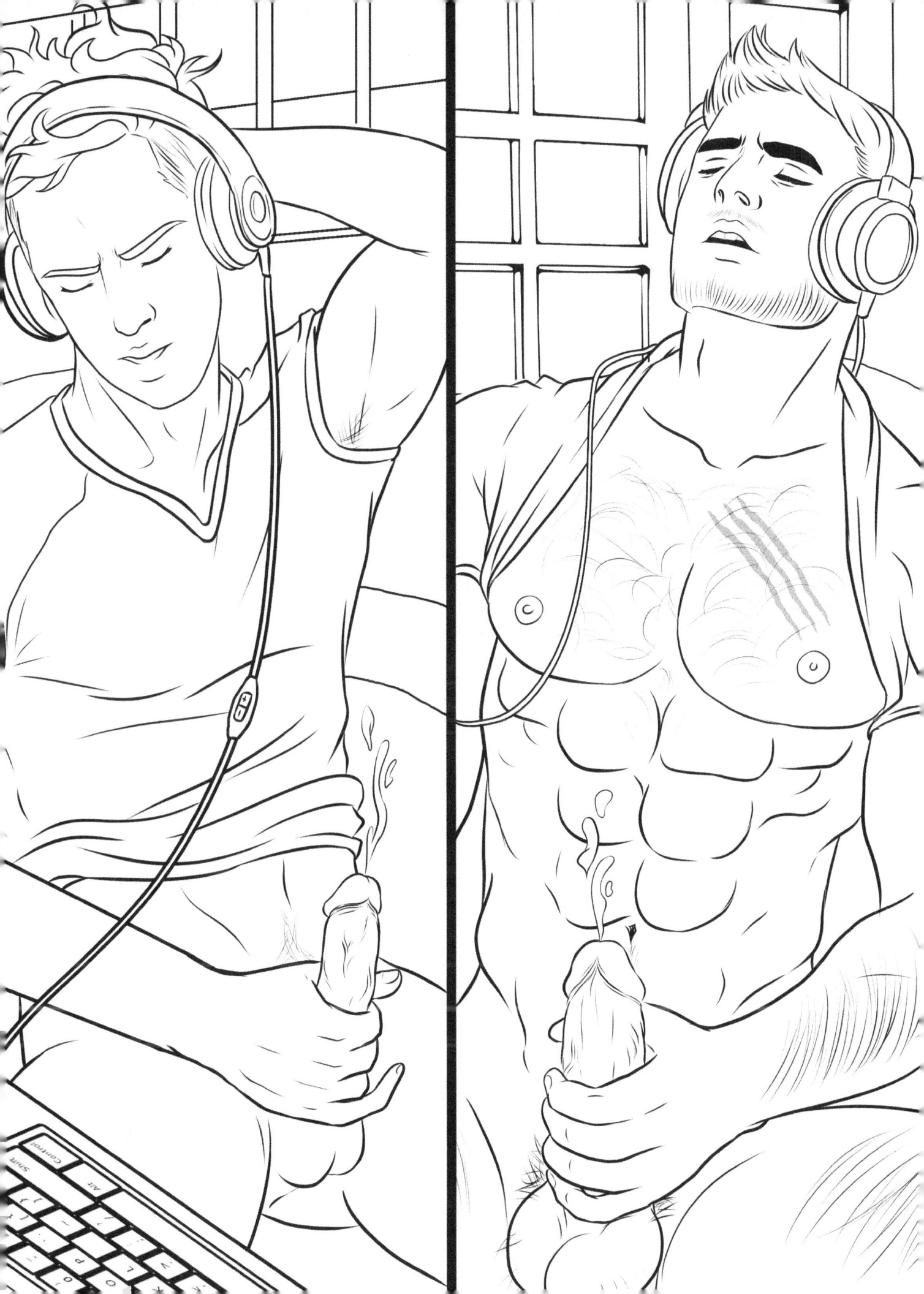

I should probably care that with every thrust and every time Owen's slammed back into the wall there's a loud thump, along with a rattle of the door that would surely cause any passersby to be curious. But I don't. I can't care about anything right now except how fucking amazing it feels to be inside this man.

I'm careful not to go too deep; this is my first time doing this, after all—I'm not about to bite off more than I can chew. But if the noises Owen's making right now, and the way he's thrashing his head about are any indication, I'm doing a pretty decent job.

VIRTUALLY SCREWED

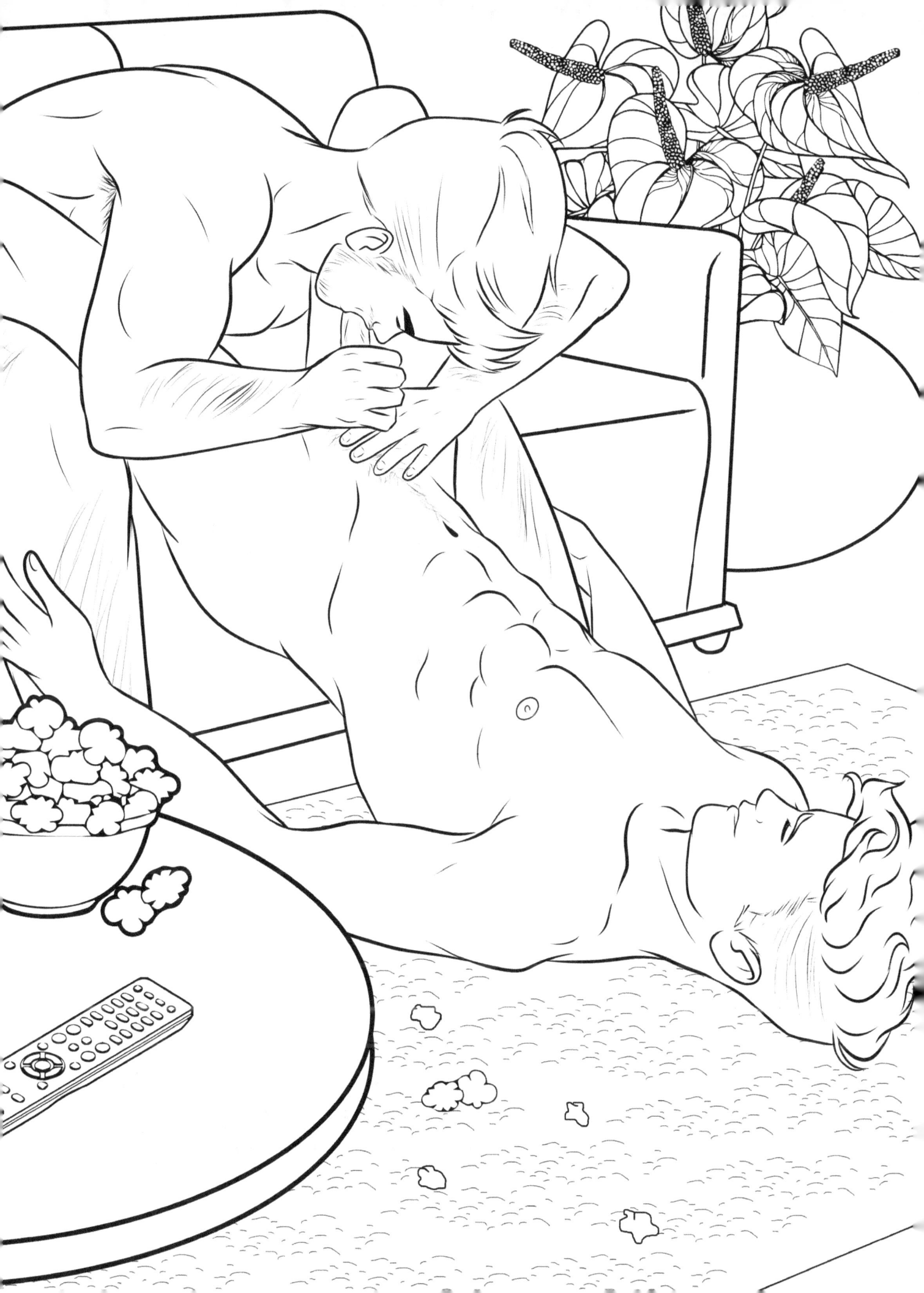

"Need a taste," is his only explanation, and he wraps his mouth around my throbbing dick. I dig my fingers into Owen's ass as he thrusts his own cock in and out of my mouth; I take it all willingly, eagerly, his enthusiasm and need for me the most incredible turn on you can imagine.

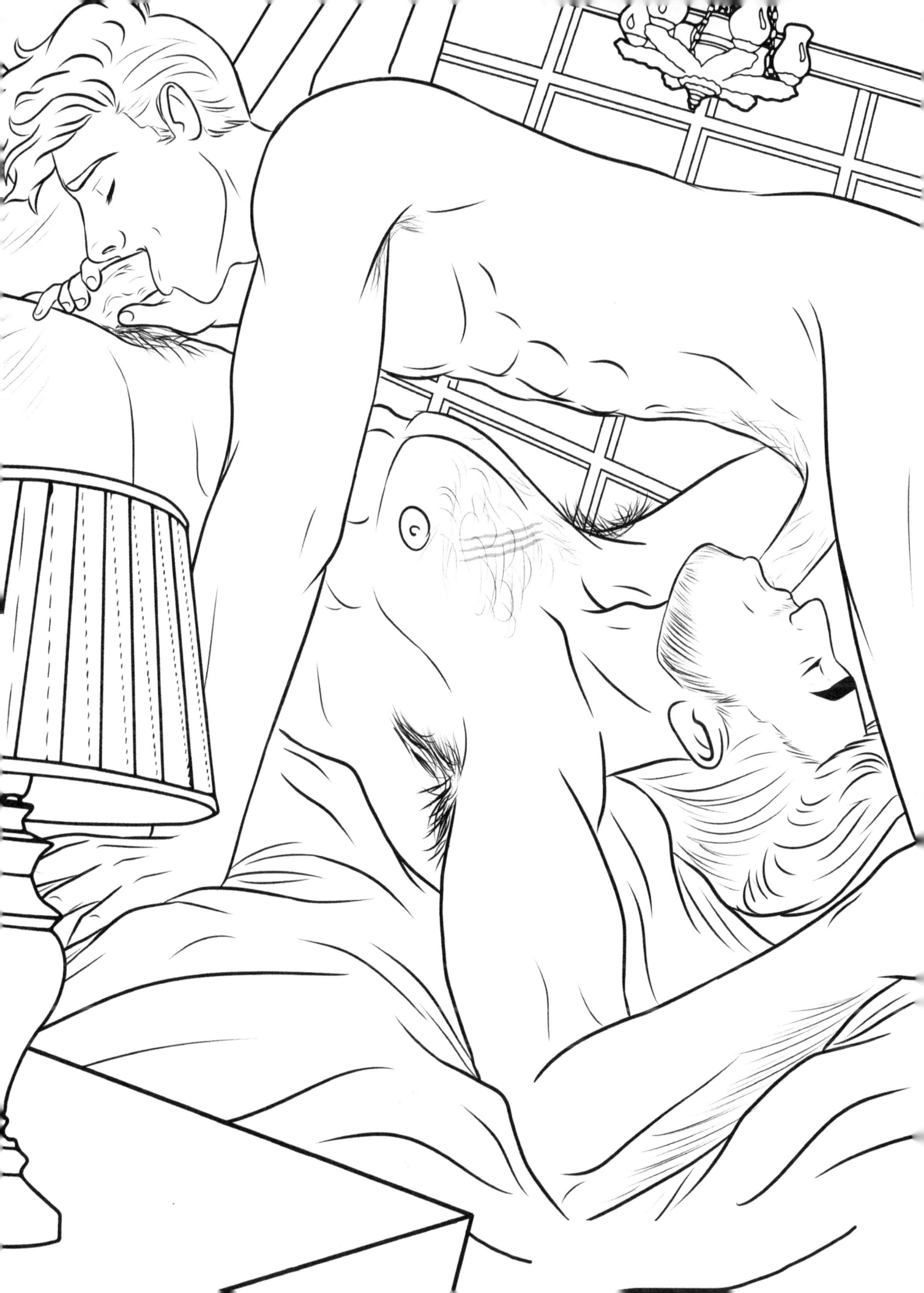

As I slowly slide down, his thick cock filling me inch by inch, all I can think is *why?* Why the fuck could I have possibly thought I could walk away from this man? Why did I let my fear over what strangers might think about us outweigh everything I feel in my heart, in my body, in my soul?

Because I'm an idiot, that's why.

I bring my hand up to his face, cupping his cheek and guiding his lips to mine. We kiss, and for a moment I completely forget there's anyone else in the room.

"I presume you'd prefer something simple," Lukas says. "Rather than the full Orthodox ceremony?"

"Definitely simple," Owen says and I nod in agreement.

And twenty-five minutes later, the entire world disappears as I kiss my husband for the first time.

CRAZY *LITTLE* FLING

"So fucking tight. Going to feel so good around my cock."

"Well, what are you bloody waiting for, mate? Fuck me then."

CRAZY *LITTLE*
FLING

The guy's head snaps up at that, and I can see the moment he recognizes me in turn. I'm pretty sure that slack-jawed look is the same one I was wearing about ten seconds ago. He masters it pretty quickly and it's replaced by wary confusion as his eyes dart from me to Will and back again. And I know exactly what he's thinking. How bad is this situation? Did he fuck his best friend's kid? Or his best friend's kid's friend?

CRAZY *LITTLE* FLING

I'd like to state for the record that when I saw my sexy redhead again and realized who he was I didn't *intend* to sneak off to a bathroom with him after dinner and let him blow me. But I also didn't try very hard to stop it from happening.

CRAZY *LITTLE* **FLING**

There's a reason I don't usually top: it's a lot of bloody work. And I'm nothing if not a bag of lazy bones. But Shay seems to have tapped into my inner athlete and brought forth previously undiscovered depths of stamina.

CRAZY LITTLE FLING

I sit up and turn around so I'm straddling him the opposite way and wrap my hand around my straining cock. I tug the mask off the rest of the way so I can watch Jamie's face as I finish myself off, coming in a rush into his waiting mouth and down his chin.

CRAZY *LITTLE* **FLING**

I sit my ass down next to him and tug him over so he's sitting in my lap. "So, am I right to assume this is a flying visit?" I ask. "Or are you moving here permanently?"

"I want to move here permanently, but I still have five months left on my contract. I can't break it."

I run my hand over the side of his face, pressing a gentle kiss to his temple. "Five months. We can totally do five months."

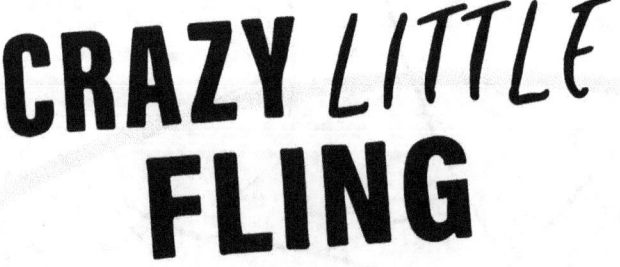

Pulling a total *Love Actually,* I drop my suitcase and race across the arrivals hall, launching myself into his arms. I cling tight to his neck and wrap my legs around his waist, not giving a shit if anyone around us thinks this is inappropriate.

CRAZY *LITTLE* FLING

Brendan and I sit at the diner talking for literally hours, and it's not until we're finally leaving that I realize we didn't even get into anything regarding the house—also known as the reason we were supposed to be meeting in the first place. I can hardly complain, though; sitting there talking to Brendan, hearing all the updates on his crazy, giant family and sharing bits and pieces of my life with him—it's the most fun I've had in a really fucking long time.

I could barely even see Wade; my vision was full of Kristi's incredible body, her tits bouncing as she rode me, her chestnut hair flowing around her shoulders. It was a stunning sight. But even with all that it was impossible to forget Wade was there. Because I could feel him *everywhere*.

Between the feel of Wade's hand stroking me, the memories still swirling from last night, and the jolt to my ego I'm getting from the way Wade's dick is responding to my touch, it takes less time than I expected for my cock to swell. It's not instantaneous, but it's pretty quick all the same, and before I really have time to process what's happening I'm hard, and I'm holding a thick, heavy cock in my hand.

After several minutes of fingering himself, Wade removes his hand and slathers some lube on the dildo. He then lines it up with his hole and I watch completely mesmerized as he pushes it inside.

I can honestly say I've never envisioned a scenario where I'd wind up with my dick in another guy's mouth. But if I had, I never would have imagined it would be this fucking hot.

HOPELESS
BROMANTICS

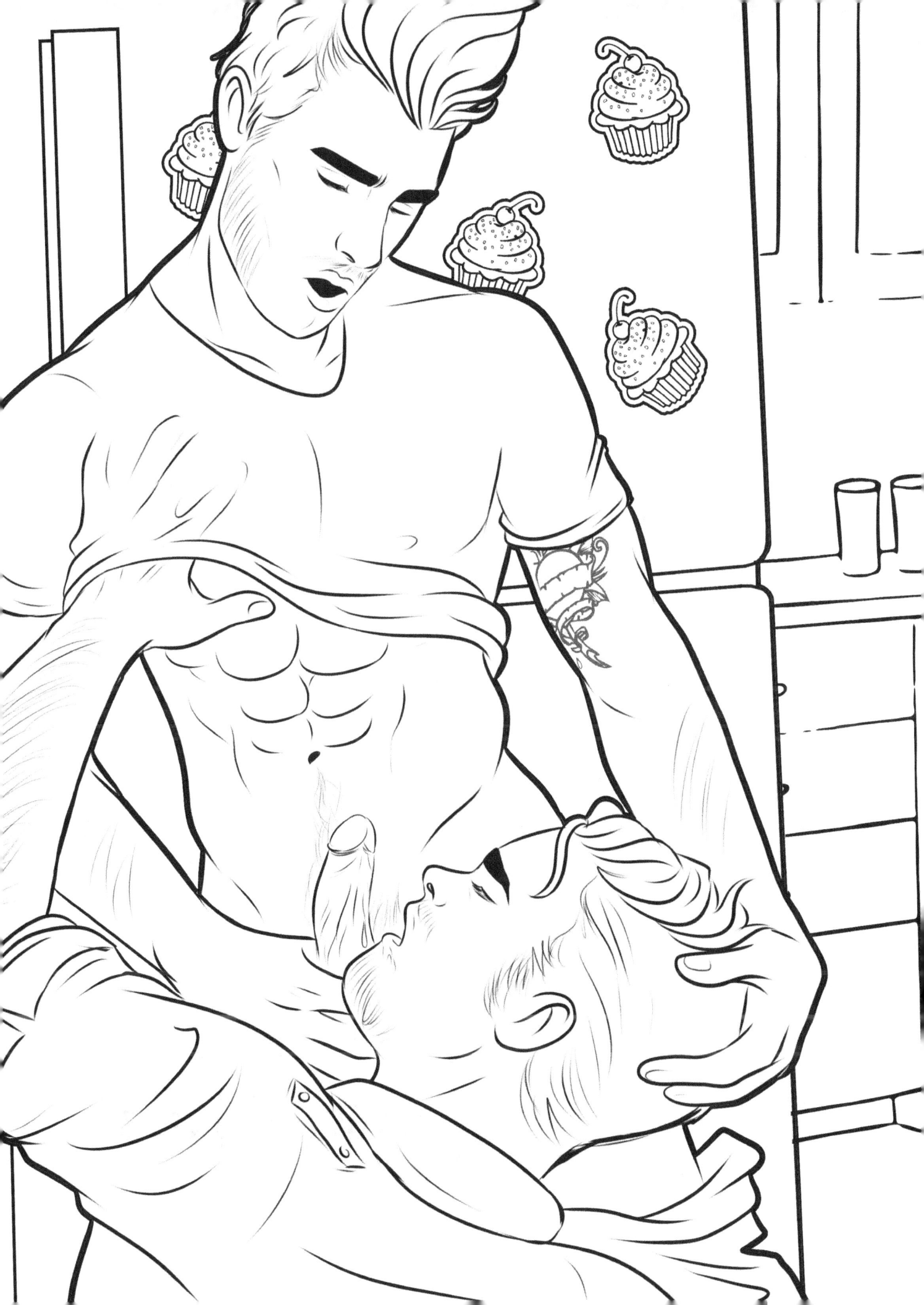

All the times I imagined being inside Brendan, I never could have dreamed it would feel this incredible. My cock is completely enveloped by his tight heat, and the way he's moving up and down and swiveling around is causing my head to just about to explode.

HOPELESS
BROMANTICS

Once Baxter is ready for bed and settled at Brendan's side with his chosen book, I press a kiss to his blond head and say goodnight. I'm about to leave the room when he calls after me. "Daddy, can Santa bring me a brother or a sister?"

HOPELESS
BROMANTICS

The problem is, once his lips touch mine I can't seem to bring myself to pull away. Instead, I open my mouth and deepen the kiss, slipping my tongue in to twine with his.

TWO MEN
and a **BABY**

Chase continues to fuss for a minute, but then he settles against Connor's chest, nestling against him like a koala. And I'm left kind of regretting suggesting Connor pick Chase up, because Connor on any normal day is pretty damn sexy, but Connor with his baby son in his arms? Damn near irresistible.

TWO MEN and a BABY

I chose this position because I figured it'd be easier for Connor his first time out if I did most of the work; I should have known he wouldn't let that fly, though. He's as intense and commanding with anal sex as he is with everything else.

TWO MEN
and a **BABY**

"Is that why you were waiting to tell them about Chase?" Josh asks as he reads through the family chat on my phone. "Because you thought you might need the distraction?"

"Possibly," I say with a teasing smile.

TWO MEN
and a BABY

He lets out a harsh, strangled groan, followed by the stream of babbled curses that I'm becoming so wonderfully familiar with. And it just encourages me to go harder, because I know he can take everything I have to give him.

TWO MEN
and a **BABY**

We stay there for a little while, me wrapped tight around Connor's body and him still buried inside me as we gather our breath.

He presses a soft kiss to my lips before resting his forehead to mine. "Do you know the song "In My Life"?" he whispers.

I'm a little thrown because a) I wasn't expecting a music quiz at the end of this epic fuck, and b) I'm still pretty out of it from the epic fuck. But as my brain starts to clear a little I realize I do know the answer to this one.

"Yeah. It's a Beatles song, right?"

He nods. As if it would be anyone else. "It's you. That song is you. For me."

As he licks around the head and down my shaft, I get little tickles from his tongue ring and oh my fucking god. The feel of that little metal ball sliding against my cock has become a familiar sensation, just like the feel of his piercing when he's inside me, and the pleasure they provide is like nothing I could have imagined before. But it's not just the piercings that do it; it's the fact it's Connor.

TWO MEN and a **BABY**

CAN'T GET YOU
OUT OF MY BED

I push my ass back against him in invitation, repeating the motion several times as he lets out curses under his breath. "Come on, baby, fuck me. You know how I like it."

CAN'T GET YOU
OUT OF MY BED

The groans of pleasure and the words of appreciation falling from his lips have to be the sweetest sounds I've ever heard. And the creaking of the bull as it rocks a little with every hard thrust has to be a close second.

I don't wait to hear the but. I just wrap my hands around his face and draw his lips to mine. I'm relieved when he doesn't hesitate, instead he wraps his arms around my waist and opens his mouth to deepen the kiss.

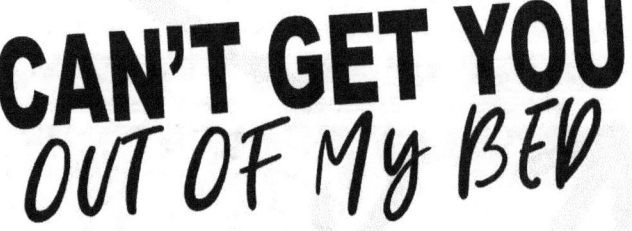

Once I catch his gaze I find it impossible to look away. The emotion swirling in those jade green eyes is just so . . . overwhelming. There's vulnerability, and hope, and regret, and pain, and . . . love. It's like everything I've ever felt for this man is being reflected right back at me. And as I listen to the lyrics he's singing, as badly performed as they are, I can't help feeling like every single line has been written specifically for us.

Is it cheesy to say being inside Ben like this, feeling his body wrapped tight around my cock, knowing there's nothing between us, feels like home? Yeah, that's super cheesy. But whatever, I don't care.

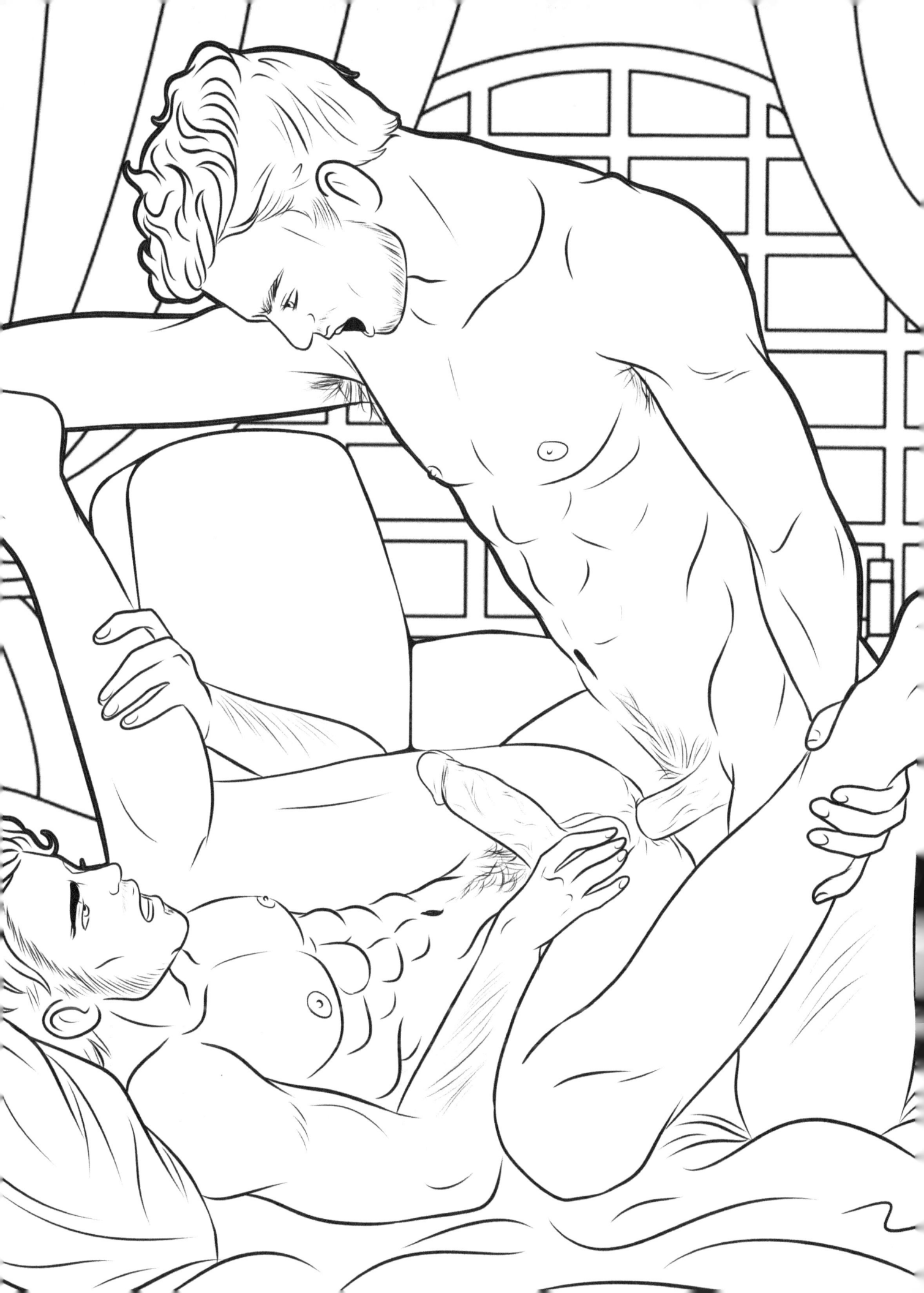

"Oh, god, I'm going to have to get used to this, aren't I?" Ellie says.

"You have ten seconds to make yourself scarce before I drop to the floor and start sucking Ben off," Aidan tells her.

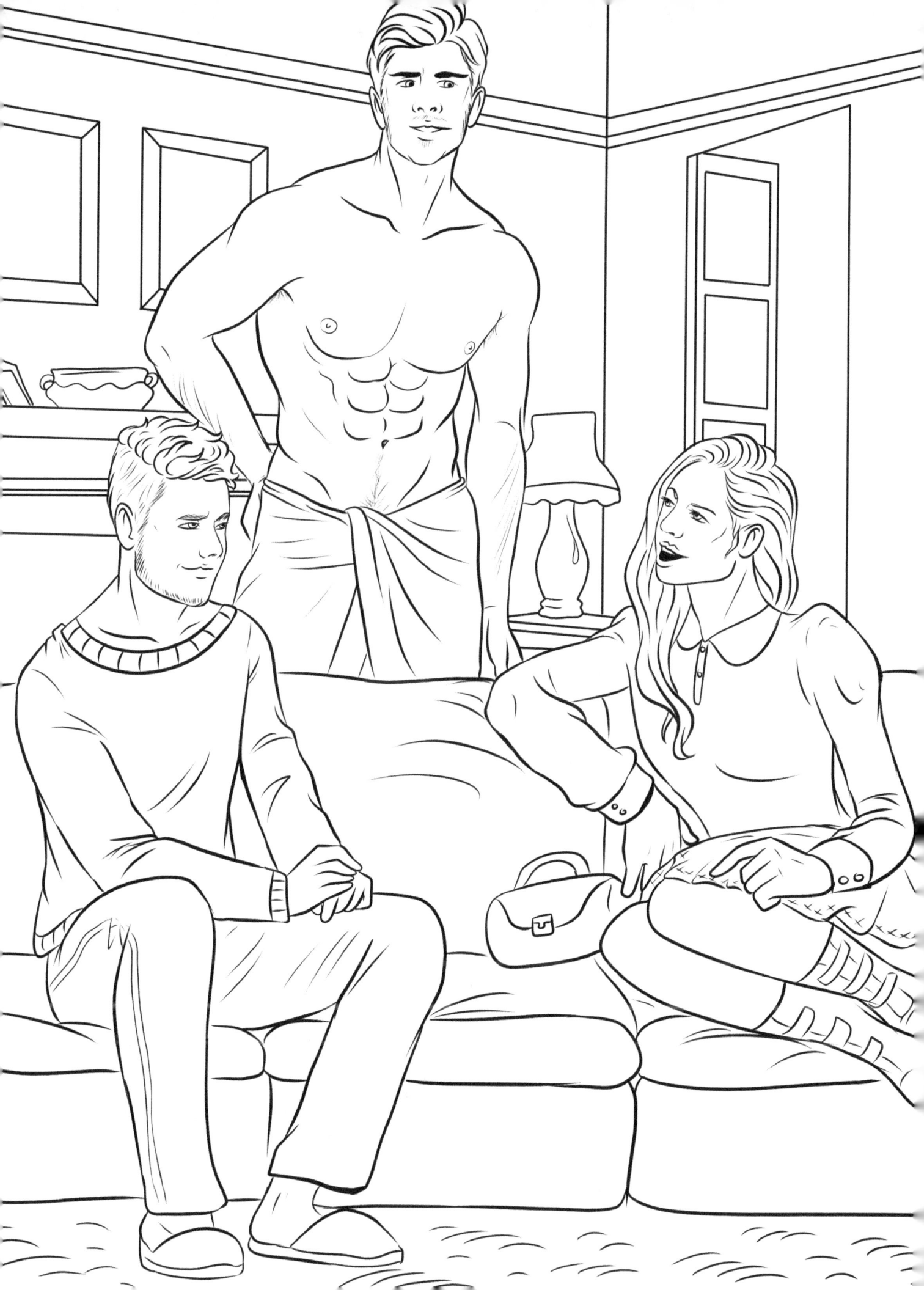

I love all the sex we have, but there's something extra special about this. It's something about the way I can just give up all my power and know without a shadow of a doubt I'm safe in Ben's hands. It's heady, and intoxicating, and just so fucking hot.

CAN'T GET YOU
OUT OF MY BED

O COME,
ALL YE KELLYS

Her gaze slowly travels up and down my body and then she draws in a deep breath, letting it out slowly. Narrowing her eyes at me, she says, "If you thought coming here smelling like a rainforest and wearing a sweater so thin it hides literally none of your abs would break me . . . you were mistaken."

O COME,
ALL YE KELLYS

With a kind of feverish delight, Baxter rips in to present after present, becoming more and more excited as each new gift reveals itself: a slime-making kit, Avengers Legos, a balance board, several new books.

O COME,
ALL YE KELLYS

MERRY christmas

"Oh my god! Oh my god, he's walking!" Connor exclaims.

Yeah, not exactly. That one tiny non-step is pretty much all Chase can manage right now, and he topples over onto his backside, his arms still held out toward Connor.

O COME,
ALL YE KELLYS

"I love that you proposed with glitter and a purple ring," I say, grinning against his lips.

O COME,
ALL YE KELLYS

I find Ben's hand under the table, giving it a squeeze. In the months since we moved to Austin I haven't regretted one second. I love seeing how happy Ben is here, especially when he's with his family. I wouldn't go back on my decision to move here for anything.

O COME,
ALL YE KELLYS

I take Ryder's hand and lead him toward the living room. "Do you like coloring, Ryder? We have some crayons over here."

O COME,
ALL YE KELLYS

The next day, we're able to bring little Caplin home to our apartment, where he has a very successful first meeting with Bucky.

O COME, ALL YE KELLYS

www.ingramcontent.com/pod-product-compliance
Lightning Source LLC
Chambersburg PA
CBHW082059090726
47909CB00011B/3085